# Caresaway

# Caresaway

DJ Cockburn

AnnorlundaBooks

Cover design by Thomas Dorman.

Editing services from Nerine Dorman.

Copyright © 2017 DJ Cockburn.

Published in the United States by Annorlunda Books.

Queries: info@annorlundaenterprises.com

First Edition

ISBN-13: 978-1-944354-19-0

Edward Crofte strode through the door marked 'CEO' without knocking. He'd been looking forward to doing that for a long time. He stood in the middle of the room until Anthony D'Olivera looked up from the papers he was packing into a box.

Back in the bad old days, Edward would have been able to interpret D'Olivera's expression instantly. Now he was less certain, but as long as he could see defeat, he knew all he needed to.

"Come to mark your new territory?" D'Olivera's Cape Flats accent, normally no more than a hint in his vowels, was clear even to Edward's English ears.

Edward strolled to the plate glass window where he looked down at Buitengracht Street, carving through Cape Town toward the cloud pouring off Table Mountain like some impossibly huge waterfall. An open-topped Maserati turned left out of Buitengracht on to Strand Street. With his CEO's salary, he'd be able to afford one for himself. Or at least persuade the bank to extend his credit far enough.

"Come on, Anthony," he said. "It's not like that. Most of our profit comes from Caresaway, so you can't blame the board if they think you're holding up the marketing."

Edward didn't look around, but he could feel D'Olivera's eyes on the back of his neck.

"And Caresaway's your baby, right?" asked D'Olivera.

"Well yes, actually, it is." That might have been a gloat too far. "Though of course, it was you who brought it on board. And me with it."

"Hm." D'Olivera's single syllable carried years of regret. He couldn't know the details of the boardroom alliance Edward had built against him, but twenty minutes ago he'd felt the result in the no-confidence vote.

"We're in the middle of a global recession, Anthony. We need to make the most of our one blockbuster product."

"So you said in the board meeting. Repeatedly. But does it bother you that the product may be *why* we're in the middle of a global recession?"

"No."

Edward turned at D'Olivera's sigh.

"Do you remember who you used to be, Edward?" asked D'Olivera. "The day you told me about Caresaway?"

"I was a failure. A victim. Now I'm a CEO. Works for me."

"You struck me as a man of ideals and compassion. You genuinely wanted Caresaway to help people."

"It has. I've given the world its only effective antidepressant. It's helped a lot of people. If I've done well out of it, I've earned it."

"But you never meant it to become a corporate aid, did you? Now everyone who wants to make it in business is popping them like they used to snort cocaine. Look at you. You were the first to kill your soul with the stuff. Now you stand there smirking, but we both know this isn't really you."

Edward rolled his eyes at the metaphysical nonsense. If he'd ever had a soul, whatever that was, it hadn't been doing him much good.

"Believe what you like, Anthony," he said. "It may help you adjust to retirement."

D'Olivera turned away. Very few people could match gazes with Edward Crofte. A couple of seconds was all it took them to recognize the power behind his eyes. Making people look away was one of the little pleasures that made it worth getting out of bed in the morning.

A knock sounded on the door.

"Come in," said Edward, before D'Olivera could react.

Beatrice Tshabalala, D'Olivera's PA, sidled in as though she feared stepping on a snake hiding in the carpet.

"Anthony? We've just heard," she said. "I'm so sorry."

"Thank you, Beatrice," said D'Olivera.

She hugged him. As she stepped away, she darted a look at Edward. Edward met her eyes. She looked away, so she didn't see him sneer. Her creaseless trouser suit, her immaculate cornrows, her understated makeup - everything about her screamed 'take me seriously' - but one glance was enough to tell her where the power in the room lay. She could try to hide from it in the sentimental look she was sharing with D'Olivera but she knew. Prey could always recognize a predator.

"Anthony, I've sent someone to get some drinks in. We'd really like you to join us when you've finished," she said.

"Thank you, Beatrice. That's very thoughtful," said D'Olivera. "I'll come down now. I'm sure Edward isn't in such a hurry to move in, and the company downstairs would be a little more to my liking."

Cheeky sod. Still, no harm in a show of magnanimity.

"Go right ahead," Edward said. "As long as I can move my stuff in by tomorrow morning."

D'Olivera and Beatrice walked into the open-plan admin office outside the CEO's office. People left their desks to shake D'Olivera's hand and follow him to the drinks party. This must be what a lion felt watching a herd of wildebeest.

Edward noticed an anomaly. The pretty blond intern was deviating from the herd and moving in his direction. Lisa, that was her name.

She stopped at the open door and put a hand on it as though it was a physical barrier. Her hips swayed, revealing both her nervousness and her confidence that she could always get by with the right look at the right person. If he hadn't already slept with her, Edward would have found it irresistible. As he'd already had her a couple of times, it was merely tempting.

"Hi," she said.

He said nothing.

"I've just heard. It's wonderful news."

"Yes, thank you." Her smile didn't quite hit the confident flirting she was aiming for. Edward frowned to make it more difficult for her. It might be amusing to see how hard she'd try.

"Does that mean you'll take me to a more expensive restaurant tonight?" she asked.

Full marks for effort. But why not? She had that brand of luscious you could only find in well-to-do girls who were still experimenting with adulthood. It withered away by the time they hit twenty-three or twenty-four.

"I'll pick you up at seven," he said. "But for now, you'd better go for drinks with everyone else."

"Okay. See you then."

She was, after all, one of the herd. In a week or so, she wouldn't even be that. She'd fade to bland after another date or two, and he understood safe sex at work. Only with temps and interns who could be fired without repercussion when he got bored with them.

He sat in D'Olivera's high-backed chair and put his feet up on the desk. Childish? Perhaps, but he was going to enjoy this office. He'd have to get rid of this chair and change the carpet; let people know the new regime would be different. No more first naming in here. He'd be Doctor Crofte or there'd be trouble.

No whining about killing souls and who he used to be when he didn't have a high-backed chair, which was what mattered. He'd been a pretty sorry specimen when he met D'Olivera, but that was a blip. It was absurd to think he'd made it here because of a few pills, even if they were his own invention. A man like him would always find his own level.

He could stop taking the pills right now and he'd still be Doctor Edward Crofte, inventor of Caresaway and CEO of Pharmakaap. Not Ed the unshaven of the drafty flat somewhere near Cambridge. D'Olivera had talked as though he were addicted, like the miserable wrecks on the streets, their lives devoted to the next puff of tik. He took the blister pack of Caresaway out of his pocket and threw it in the waste basket. He felt no need to retrieve it. He wasn't an addict. He could never take another Caresaway pill and he'd still belong in the high-backed chair. Never be the pathetic excuse for a man he'd been the day he met D'Olivera.

■■■■■■

His memories of that day were colored by the misery that had become his daily companion.

Tia had been there for him. She always was.

When she said, "You've got a face like the weather," she made it sound as though his frown was unusual.

Edward watched rain hammer the window of the franchise café. November in Cambridgeshire matched his mood.

"Do you blame me?" he asked. "Pfizer, GSK and Sanofi have all told us they need to see a trial of at least five hundred people. Where are we going to get the cash for that?"

They couldn't, which Tia knew as well as he did. They shared both the directorship of the startup company that developed Caresaway and the mortgage arrears on their flat.

She took his hand.

"Edki, look at me." It was a ritual, but they followed it because her touch drained at least some of the tension from his shoulders. When they'd started the company, they'd been partners in all senses of the word. Now he depended on Tia to carry both him and Caresaway.

"I love you," she said. "You're the most brilliant man I know, and the most compassionate, and I wouldn't be here with you if I didn't really believe you'd got something when you came up with Caresaway."

He loved her for saying it. He despised himself for needing to hear it.

"*We* came up with Caresaway. We wouldn't have a company if you hadn't worked out how to synthesize it in bulk." He looked down. "Though we might be able to afford the mortgage."

"Now enough of that." She exaggerated her accent, knowing he found it sexy. "Caresaway's better than any antidepressant on the market at the moment. Let's not lose sight of that."

Her voice rang with conviction, which wasn't purely for his benefit. She was talking about what really mattered to her - not the money, but the possibility that Caresaway might help people navigate the darkest times in their lives. He hated himself all over again because her desire to help was no longer abstract, as it had been when they'd started. She'd spent three years watching the man she loved sinking into the depression they were trying to cure.

"Pharmakaap isn't one of the old-school bigshots who want the product gift wrapped before they'll get off their arse and look at it," said Tia. "The CEO got on a plane to England because he wants to move on from making generic drugs and own a few patents."

Edward glanced at his watch.

"You've got time to drink your latte," she said.

Edward sipped his coffee and followed it with a mouthful of cheesecake. He was living on caffeine and comfort food, and it was beginning to show around his middle. Tia must have noticed, but she never mentioned it.

"Tell me about the CEO. This guy D'Olivera," he said. "You met him?"

"He was one of my tutors at uni. He should take us a bit more seriously than if he'd never heard of either of us."

"I don't know when he went corporate," she said. "He's Cape Coloured like me, but he's got a bit more milk in his coffee."

Edward put down his latte. "What's that mean?"

"His skin's a bit lighter and he speaks English almost like a white person. These things matter when you grow up on the Cape Flats."

"If you say so. One day, you'll have to take me there so I can understand properly. Right now, all I know is I'll never stop being grateful to the man if he buys us out."

"Actually, I rather like that you don't understand, but tell me again why Caresaway's a good drug. Pretend I'm D'Olivera. Try to sound like you mean it this time."

"Oh, you know, full recovery from depression in eighteen of twenty cases in a week. Enough to make the bloke from Pfizer give us his most skeptical frown."

"That's because you were mumbling. Now tell me about the complete lack of nasty side effects."

"Ah…"

"Ah? What do you mean, ah?"

"I mean…do you remember a couple of spouses said they were concerned about behavior changes?"

"I remember that woman who said her husband had been neglecting her since he was on the pills. I thought she was a bit of a control freak. Liked her man better when he was needy."

"It crossed my mind too, but it bothered me enough to ask a few questions during follow-up visits."

Edward stuffed a lump of cheesecake into his mouth.

"And? Stop stalling, Edki. You can finish the cake in a minute."

Edward swallowed. "It bothered me enough that I asked an old friend. A psychologist. He had a word with one or two of them."

"One or two?"

Edward pushed the rest of the cheesecake around the plate with his fork. He wanted to eat it but he recognized the way Tia's eyebrows pressed together. He only spoke imprecisely if he was being evasive, and she knew it. Last time had been when he tried to deal with a technician who had been late every day for a month, and he'd come out of the disciplinary meeting to tell Tia he might possibly have been thinking about lending her some money.

"Five."

"Five." Tia's voice was so quiet he could hardly hear it.

Her furrowed brow showed she understood there was a problem she'd have to draw out of him, and how much it hurt that he hadn't told her until they were about to meet a potential buyer. He wanted to curl up and hide from her, the world and above all, himself. It was only when he screwed up like this that he saw how much of a burden he was to her.

Her pause told him she was fighting down her irritation so she could focus on the problem. When she spoke, her voice was level but the furrows were still there.

"About a quarter of the ones who got Caresaway," she said. "What did he say about them?"

"They all scored at least thirty-three on the Hare test."

Tia looked blank. "Edki." She took the fork out of his hand.

"Okay. Right. Well, if you score above thirty on the Hare test, you're technically a psychopath."

Tia drew back. She tilted her head, the way she did when he was about to deliver the punchline to one of his more labored jokes.

"A psycho? As in Hannibal Lecter?"

"What? No, no, that's all Hollywood. Real psychopaths aren't particularly interested in violence. They're self-absorbed, dishonest and have a complete lack of empathy, but they're not violent. Well, most of them aren't, anyway."

"That's something. So *most* of our subjects won't be going on a killing spree."

"No. But a lot of psychopaths end up in prison for one thing or another. Or they do well as business executives."

"Are you serious?"

"Yes, it seems being manipulative and lacking empathy get you a long way in office politics."

"Oh great. So we've made a must-have accessory for the next Bernie Madoff."

"It's not funny, Tia. These people have lost a lot more than their depression."

"No it isn't funny." Tia closed her eyes and took a breath.

Edward loved that look. It meant she was working toward a solution.

"Is it possible we just happened to recruit a bunch of psychopaths as our treatment group?" she asked.

"No. Less than one in a hundred people are psychopaths, so it's not likely we randomly picked up five of them. Anyway, psychopaths don't get depressed. It's part of the disorder."

"So it sort of makes sense that making someone a psychopath might cure their depression."

"Yes, but I can't understand how it happened. Psychopathy's hardwired. It can't be induced or cured. It's to do with the function of the amygdala—"

"Edki. We can discuss specifics later. Right now, we have half an hour before you present to Pharmakaap, so the question is how much we tell them. Look, this wasn't part of the study protocol, was it? Getting your pal to have a word with a few test subjects is hardly scientific data."

"Well, no."

"We need to test all of them, and test them again when they come off Caresaway. By the time we've done that, we'll probably find we're barking up the wrong tree."

Edward couldn't argue with that. He'd learned years ago that if the first observations suggested dramatic conclusions, they were usually averaged away in the complete dataset. Tia was probably right and he was worrying over nothing. Again.

It was going to be okay. Tia was developing a plan. He chased the cheesecake around the plate with his fork, wishing he'd thought of that himself. Once he'd identified the problem, he'd felt as if it were a brick wall in front of him. He'd been more worried about how to tell Tia than about solving it.

"So we'll call your friend tomorrow," she said. "Right now, we need to focus on the presentation."

Edward looked down. It was as if the marbled chocolate cheesecake on his plate commanded his attention.

"Oh, will you just eat the bloody cake," said Tia. "You're staring at it like a starving puppy."

Her tone reminded him that she was under as much pressure as he was, even if she handled it so much better.

Edward shoveled the last of the cheesecake into his mouth without tasting it.

"So your presentation just says eighteen out of twenty cured with no adverse events."

"Mm."

"So present what we've verified and we'll chase up the psychopath business later."

Edward swallowed the cake. "We can't just pretend it didn't happen."

"No, we can't. But Pharmakaap aren't looking for a finished product. If we find Caresaway really causes psychopathy, we can adjust the dose regime. We can go right back to the formulation if we have to, but only with Pharmakaap paying us to do it. We can't afford to keep going on our own. If we really can't fix it, we'll market it with a warning and make sure it isn't approved for more than a few weeks at a time. Thinking about it, it's no worse than the side effects of a lot of antidepressants on the market, and none of them cure depression like Caresaway. I know I'd rather have you being a bit of a psychopath for a while than…well."

She didn't need to finish. He was as depressed as anyone they recruited into the trial.

"So the question," she said, "is whether there's any reason to mention this to D'Olivera."

"I don't…" Edward closed his eyes and shook his head. He couldn't get his thoughts in order these days. "No."

"Neither can I," she said. "So just blow them away with the data. You sell Caresaway to Pharmakaap and we can forget about overdue mortgage payments and your bloody English weather." She waved at the rain-lashed window.

"Just think of you and me, on the beach at Clifton, watching the whales go past. Sound good?"

"Yes." There was no arguing with that. "Yes, it does."

"Good. Now I'm going to the ladies' and you get your head together. Think through what you're going to say one last time and we'll go."

As she stood, she kissed his lips and slid a hand into his crotch for a quick squeeze. She drew back and met his eyes.

"Okay?"

"Okay."

He sank his head into his hands. No, he wasn't "okay." He hadn't even responded to her squeeze. It wasn't so long ago that all she had to do was raise an eyebrow in that particular way of hers to get him going. Now it was months since they'd had sex. He'd failed at being a man as well as a businessman.

He fingered the blister pack of Caresaway in his pocket, ready to pass around in the presentation. Tia said people were more likely to believe in something they could hold in their hand than in pixels on a screen.

"Caresaway," he tested the word Tia had coined.

It was a bad joke. When his employers at Cambridge University showed no interest in patenting the compound he'd identified, the opportunity to base a startup around it had been too good to miss. Three years of undiluted stress later, he wished he'd never thought of the stuff.

Not for the first time, it occurred to him that he might be holding the solution in his hand. If Caresaway was as good an antidepressant as he was about to tell Pharmakaap, it was exactly what he needed. And it was that good. The data said so.

He held the pack in front of him.

No, he couldn't. It was still unproven.

He'd fed it to twenty people. He couldn't do that and then decide he was too afraid to feed it to himself.

The psychopath effect might be real.

Then he'd stop taking it. Tia had all but said she'd rather he was psychopathic than depressed. That, he realized, was the real reason she didn't want to believe in a side effect. She was exhausted from carrying him and the company. If Pharmakaap bought them out, he'd have a chance to recover without the pressures and frustrations of trying to sell Caresaway.

Perhaps she was right. For a moment, a ray of hope pierced the fog of his mind. Perhaps the data really could persuade D'Olivera to buy Caresaway. All their debts would be cleared at a stroke. Another thought reasserted his gloom. Tia's finances would no longer be tied to his. She'd have one less reason to carry his emotional dependence. He was sure she hadn't thought of that, but how many more screw-ups could he expect her to put up with? He was a man-shaped open wound that she tried to kiss better without touching in the wrong way.

Yet if D'Olivera didn't buy them out, how long would Tia go on dedicating herself to the twin lost causes of Edward and Caresaway? Either way, he'd lose her.

He'd lose Tia.

Oh, what the hell?

He pushed a pill out of the pack and washed it down with the last of his latte.

The pills were back in his pocket when Tia came back. He stood. She straightened his tie.

"Ready, Edki?"

"I'll have to be." He was ready.

He gave the best presentation of his life. D'Olivera invited him to Cape Town to give it to Pharmakaap's main investors.

He might have wondered how things would have worked out if he'd stammered and mumbled as he had with Pfizer, but by the time Pharmakaap had actually bought Caresaway, such introspective questions no longer occurred to him.

■■■■■■

Driving to work in a fire engine red Maserati for the first time should have filled Edward with undiluted joy. When he gunned the engine, the crackle of pistons engineered with uniquely Italian precision echoed around Cape Town. Heads turned toward a man reveling in his just deserts.

So what was the itch in the back of his mind? The sense that something wasn't as it should be? It had been following him around for the past few days. As he pulled into the car park beneath the office block, he sensed something ominous was lurking in the shadow while his eyes adjusted. Ridiculous. He was too rational for superstition, and if anything was amiss, he could handle it.

He growled the Maserati into his parking space. Even the sound the door made when closing shouted style. A guard strode from behind a van, on his way back to the security booth.

"You!" Edward shouted. "I see one scratch on this car, you're fired!"

The man snapped to attention. "*Oui, monsieur!*"

Half the security guards in Cape Town were Congolese. The bloody man probably hadn't understood a word Edward said. Perhaps that was why watching a man snap to attention at his words didn't give him the thrill it usually did.

It cheered him to see the hive of industry in the admin office. If the activity only started when he stepped out of the lift, it showed his people knew their place and, more importantly, knew his.

He walked to the window, looking at the peak of Lion's Head with the path scarred into its green flanks as it wound its way to the top. He followed the steep slope as it swept down to the azure Atlantic.

It was beautiful.

The thought surprised him. Natural beauty wasn't something he'd appreciated for years. If he stood at the window every morning, it was because he wanted to have his back to the door two minutes later.

The click and scuff of it opening was right on cue.

"Your coffee, sir."

Beatrice's voice sounded as wary as usual. She was a good PA and Edward planned to keep her, but he wanted to knock any residual loyalty to D'Olivera out of her.

He heard the mug tap down on his desk. He waited, but he didn't hear the door close behind her.

"Doctor Crofte?"

"Mm."

Suddenly it all felt petty. Did he have nothing better to do than torment a woman who must have got the message by now? He turned around.

Beatrice was as well-groomed as always, but the rings under her eyes startled him. They looked like ground zero in a devastated soul. He felt something. Something he hadn't felt for a long time, but he must have felt it before because he recognized it even if he couldn't remember what it was called.

"Sit down, Beatrice," he said. "We need to talk."

She sat with her back ramrod straight. Her hands clutched each other in her lap.

"Don't worry," he said. "I'm not going to fire you."

Her shoulders slid back as she let in her breath. Perhaps he'd been overdoing the dominant act with her.

When did he start thinking of it as an act?

"You're good at what you do," he said. "I'd be a fool to let you go."

Her eyes widened. No wonder she was surprised. It was as close to a compliment as he'd given anyone since he'd joined Pharmakaap. He looked again and saw more fear than surprise. That didn't make sense. Why would she be afraid?

Oh.

Was this what he'd come to? He couldn't say something nice without her thinking he was making a pass at her?

If that was what she thought, why did he care?

"Is everything else all right, Beatrice? You look a little, well, unhappy."

It sounded lame, but he hoped she'd get the message that he didn't expect a blowjob.

Her mouth twitched, trying for a professional smile. She looked as if she was about to get up and leave, releasing them both from an awkward moment. She cuffed at a tear fleeing down her cheek. She pressed her hand to her mouth to stifle the sob jerking her shoulders.

Edward was sitting as bolt upright as she was. He had no idea what to say or do.

"I'm sorry, Doctor Crofte," she said. "It won't happen again. I'm fine."

"No, you're not." He regretted the words as soon as they were out of his mouth, but he couldn't unsay them now. "Do you want to tell me about it?"

He hoped she'd say no. He really wanted her to say no.

"I have HIV," she said. "I found out a week ago. My husband got pneumonia so we were both tested. We're both positive and...and..."

Her voice broke. "So is our son."

Edward hadn't thought much about HIV before he moved to Cape Town, but below the Sahara it was the bogeyman lying in wait for the unwary. He was an obsessive condom user, but it was still hard to shake the sense of being one routine test away from the sky falling in.

Beatrice dug some tissues out of her jacket pocket and blew her nose. If she had tissues in her pocket, she'd expected to go for a cry in the toilets, which should have been reason enough to fire her. Over her shoulder, he saw people in the admin office gawping through the window. Two weeks of putting his own stamp on the place were unraveling but he couldn't find it in himself to do what needed to be done. All he felt was that thing he suddenly found the name for—pity.

"Your husband," he said. "Is he…I mean, how is he?"

"I guess he's okay. As soon as he got out of hospital, he accused me of infecting him and went back to Durban. He's the only man I ever…"

Her voice disintegrated into sobs, punctuated with, "I'm sorry, I'm sorry."

She took a deep breath and blew her nose. To Edward's relief, she seemed to be pulling herself together.

"I'm very sorry, Doctor Crofte." Her voice was level again. "From now on, I won't bring my personal problems to work."

"No, No, I… what's your CD4 count, Beatrice?"

It was easier to focus on practicalities than emotions, but as soon as the words were out of his mouth, he realized it was an inappropriate question to ask an employee.

Beatrice answered readily enough. "Eight hundred and fifty. That's okay, isn't it?"

Her question sounded genuine. Her doctor must have been less than generous with information.

"Yes, that's fine," said Edward. "But I hope they've arranged to monitor you regularly?"

She nodded.

"Good. And also your son?"

She nodded again.

Why was he asking personal questions? Back in Cambridge, he'd been drawn into people's problems enough times to know it was a mistake. It hadn't been hard to keep a safe distance recently, so what had changed?

As soon as he formed the question, the answer was obvious. Two weeks after his last Caresaway pill, he was no longer a psychopath. That was something to think about when he didn't have a woman crying in front of him.

"Doctor Crofte, I'm very, very sorry to break down like this," she said. "I promise it won't happen again."

"I understand. It's a lot to deal with."

She looked at him as though he'd sprouted a second head. Her perplexity cut him deeper than her tears. He looked away and rummaged in a desk drawer.

"You might like to try these," he said.

He handed her a half-full box of Caresaway blister packs.

Beatrice took it with her fingertips, as though it had thorns.

"It won't bite you," he said.

"I hear things," she said. "People change when they take these."

"It's true it can change your personality after a while." There was no point in denying it, although Edward had made sure the Hare tests in Cambridge had never been reported or repeated. "But there's only enough in there for three weeks. That'll get you through the hardest times. Then you stop taking them and you'll be your usual self again."

"You're sure of that?"

"Very sure." He didn't mention how sure the past few minutes had made him. "Just take them with you and think about it, okay?"

"Thank you."

"And Beatrice?" Edward may as well give up on his image. "Take the rest of the day off."

She gaped at him. He sipped the coffee to avoid looking at her. It was cold.

"There's something else," she said. "Before I go."

"Yes?"

"Have you seen this?"

She held up a copy of *Time*. He hadn't even noticed she'd brought it in.

"No. Should I have done?"

She put it on the desk. "Page seven."

She stood, looking afraid he might suddenly revert to the man she thought she knew when he saw what was lurking beneath the cover photograph of the Burj Khalifa.

"I'll have a look. Seriously, Beatrice, you should give the pills a try."

"Thank you, Doctor Crofte."

Since she'd been his PA, she'd thanked him every time she left his office. This time, he thought she meant it.

When she left, he flipped open the magazine.

Tia looked back at him from a half-page photograph. She wore the sincere expression she'd used for presenting Caresaway to potential buyers. Her hair was professionally dressed, he noticed, even as he recognized the irrelevance of the observation. What mattered was the Caresaway packet she was holding up, and the headline, 'The Pill that Caused the Recession'.

Steeling himself to read the article felt like rolling up his trousers before crawling across a floor strewn with broken glass.

'When Tia de Jongh co-invented the world's most popular antidepressant,' the article started, 'she had no idea she was creating a cadre of psychopaths who would rise to rule the corporate world.'

She must have been talking to D'Olivera. There was no other way she could know Caresaway had found its way to more executives, or aspiring executives, than depressives. The author must have done some homework as well. Apart from talking to Tia, who was given the prominence due to a partner in the original Caresaway startup, the author had found a former executive who talked about being prescribed Caresaway for executive stress and who had found himself much better at disposing of the competition when he caught scent of a promotion.

"I went from deputy branch manager to regional director in less than a year," he was quoted. "I only realized what Caresaway was doing to me when my wife burned the pills and told me what the alimony payments would be if she divorced me."

Smart woman. She'd used a threat that would get through to a psychopath. Spouses of twenty years rarely showed any more sense than his casual girlfriends, demanding 'didn't you ever love me?' or 'I thought you cared about me'. Such arguments did not penetrate a mind purged of empathy and deep emotions.

'In the innocent days of the nineties,' the article continued, 'the student drugs of choice were cannabis and ecstasy. Now students at the Harvard Business School and the London School of Economics show little interest in any drug other than Caresaway, which they obtain from various illicit sources.'

Something else that came from D'Olivera, who had been concerned enough to hire private investigators in Boston and London, where they uncovered a thriving black market in forged prescriptions. Edward had been relieved to know the executives taking Caresaway were buying the real thing from Pharmakaap rather than taking their business to a counterfeiter. D'Olivera's determination to do something about the black market had been one of the reasons behind Edward's coup.

The article became personal, describing Edward's refusal to follow up on the Hare tests after the first trial, and Tia's belief that his personality had changed when he started taking Caresaway himself. At least she hadn't mentioned their personal relationship. The writer must have decided it would weaken the case if Tia came across as a vengeful ex-girlfriend.

If Caresaway had infected the executive boards of the world's corporations with people incapable of remorse and obsessed with short-term gain, the article plowed on, was it any wonder that so many corporations were so badly managed? Accepting huge bonuses from companies they'd run into the ground was exactly the sort of behavior to be expected from what the writer called a 'squabble of psychopaths,' coining a collective term Edward feared would become part of the lexicon. Helping themselves to bonuses was probably the only thing that would distract psychopaths from stabbing each other in the back, figuratively if not usually literally. Was it any wonder the global economy was tottering when it was composed of companies subverted to the enrichment of their psychopathic directors?

Two weeks ago, Edward would have thrown the magazine across the room and found someone to shout at. Now he folded his arms on his desk and sank his head into them. Tia's voice came back to him with a clarity that plunged the red Maserati into the same shade of gray as the blue sky glowing over Table Mountain.

"Oh Edki," he heard. "Edki, Edki, Edki."

■■■■■■

The effect of Caresaway had crept up on him during the days after the first pill. Tension had ebbed from his shoulders and the grinding glass had faded from his mind. If he'd felt a little less affection for Tia, the lack had been hidden behind his revitalized libido.

When D'Olivera flew Edward to Cape Town to present to Pharmakaap's investors, Edward had projected all the confidence Tia had been trying to instill in him for years. He hadn't felt more than a slight pang of conscience when he omitted the Hare test results.

D'Olivera had looked happy and had taken him and some of the fatter wallets to dinner at the Radisson Hotel, where Edward was staying. The conversation had been polite and off-topic through most of the meal, and Edward had found time to revel in his surroundings. His experience of dining out had always been constrained by budget, and splashing out meant ambient music from Jack Johnson CDs instead of the local radio station. Eating a meal under a warm night sky while waves lapped the beach was an experience he could develop a taste for, especially when the linefish was so exquisitely grilled. He'd never eaten battered cod with the same relish again.

The novelty of the experience carried him through to the chocolate mousse before he realized how easily he'd been engaging with the conversation. Surrounded by the people who would decide his future, his intestines should have been tying themselves in knots so tight he'd hardly be able to keep down the meal, let alone enjoy it. Yet he'd been drifting in and out of conversations like a practiced social butterfly. Even when the investors talked a foreign language about hedging and arbitrage, he'd been able to formulate a pertinent question. If he hadn't understood the answer, the chance to hold forth seemed to make them happy. He wasn't sure, but some of these people may actually have liked him. At the same time, something had been missing from the conversation. D'Olivera hadn't arranged this meal so his investors could pay court to Edward.

He took a quick account to check he was only on his second glass of wine, and decided to restrict himself to the occasional sip for the rest of the evening.

When they moved to the hotel bar, D'Olivera caught his eye and opened his mouth to speak. Here it comes, thought Edward.

The waitress had interrupted him. "Can I take your drinks order?"

Edward had looked away from D'Olivera to find his eyes level with her waist. Dark tights slid up slim legs to disappear under a skirt so tight she'd have trouble walking if it was any longer. Not bad.

"Do you mind if we put it on your room tab, Edward?" asked D'Olivera. "We'll pick it up with the bill."

"Not at all," said Edward.

The waitress flashed him a smile that made him look a little closer. Sensuality radiated from her flawless skin and from the curves that pushed open her blouse. It came to him that he'd just looked her body up and down. He refocused his eyes on her face.

She arched an eyebrow.

"What's your pleasure, sir?"

"I… uh…" A drink. She was asking what he'd like to drink. "White wine, please."

She left with the orders. Edward hauled his attention away from her bottom and returned it to the people he needed to impress. He'd always been awkward with women. Since he'd been with Tia, it had been a relief to be out of the game. Yet a few days away from her and he'd regressed to a hormone-saturated teenager.

Still, the waitress had been worth a second look.

"I'm really struck by the lack of side effects," said D'Olivera. "I've never seen a drug with so few."

Edward had taken his time in answering. They'd been plying him with congenial company and good wine under a warm night sky, hoping he'd drop his guard. Every clinical trial had thrown up something that wasn't covered by the protocol, and D'Olivera had wanted to know about it before Pharmakaap committed to Caresaway.

"Yes, it surprised me too," said Edward. "I'd expected something to come up, but there was none of the usual nausea and drowsiness you get with antidepressants."

It wasn't exactly a lie. Tia had been right to doubt the Hare tests when they'd only questioned five people. If D'Olivera had wanted to know about something not covered by the protocol, he should have asked directly. It was the perfect rationalization because D'Olivera couldn't know there were any off-protocol results to ask about directly.

Edward was still new enough to Caresaway to feel the need for rationalization.

"Just remission of the depression?" asked D'Olivera.

Edward had never been much good at dissembling. He half expected the forbidden information to spill out of his mouth while his conscious mind flapped its arms as if watching a train crash. He looked into D'Olivera's honest eyes and felt no need to tell him anything.

The waitress returned with a tray of drinks. She bent forward to put his wine on the table, giving him a glimpse down her blouse. He blinked rapidly, trying to clear the image of his hand inside her red bra from his mind.

"Your room number, sir?"

She dipped her eyes and twitched her mouth. Was she inviting him to look? Edward found himself enjoying the game, even if he was probably imagining it. He looked her in the eyes and dropped his gaze in a way she couldn't miss.

"For the bill," she said.

"Two oh nine."

"Nice there?" she asked.

"Very."

She stood. "I'll see." She tipped her head slightly as though asking a question. "About putting the drinks on your tab, I mean."

"Please do."

Edward was sure she put an extra swing in her hips as she left. He smiled down at his wine. He'd enjoyed the fantasy. He wondered how much money she'd expect. Was he hoping it wasn't a fantasy?

D'Olivera was asking him something. He hadn't noticed anything other than a drinks order.

"I'm sorry," said Edward. "What were you saying?"

"I was asking about the people who'd recovered from their depression. I know all the indicators you measured showed improvement. I was wondering if anything else came up?"

"No, nothing."

That was going a bit far. D'Olivera would know there was always something that didn't quite fit expectations.

"The usual bits and pieces of course, but nothing consistent. We put it down to individual variation rather than anything to do with Caresaway."

D'Olivera nodded and sipped his beer. Edward waited for his conscience to rear up and squeeze the Hare tests out of him, but it remained silent. He examined it as he might examine a lab report. Its activity remained well below the critical threshold.

D'Olivera must have been happy with Edward's answers, because the conversation drifted on to inconsequentials. D'Olivera and the investors regaled Edward with what he would later recognize as a characteristically Capetonian enthusiasm for their region. They told him of the beauty of Cape Point and the Garden Route, and looked disappointed when he said he didn't follow rugby. When the conversation moved to the best suburbs to live, he knew they'd decided to bring him on board.

He kept his resolution to not match their drinking, so when he returned to his room, he'd only had enough to keep him from sleeping. He downed his nightly Caresaway and reflected on the events of the day. Both the presentations and the evening had gone well, and he felt better about himself than he had for years. So why did he feel something was off?

He fired up his laptop and pulled up a copy of the Hare test. Edward had never looked at it with a particular person in mind, least of all himself.

He thought back to how easily he'd avoided mentioning the Hare tests.

*Item 3. Pathological lying.*

Not that he'd done anything terrible. Caresaway had been a resounding success according to the study protocol. Hardly surprising it had been successful after all the work he'd put into it. Tia had often told him he was brilliant; it was time he started listening to her.

*Item 2. Grandiose sense of self-worth.*

He thought about how easy it was to talk to D'Olivera and the investors. He usually hated social situations and drank as a nervous reflex. At some point, he'd realize he was drunk and should have kept his mouth shut for the last half hour. Tonight, he'd felt comfortable despite being evaluated.

*Item 1. Glibness / superficial charm.*

He looked at the blister pack of Caresaway. He still felt pretty good about himself. Psychopaths usually did. It was the people around them who suffered from their disorder, which was why the Caresaway trial had missed it. He and Tia had designed the protocol to test whether the recruits were recovering from their depression and whether Caresaway was making them physically ill. They hadn't thought to check whether anyone was becoming selfish or manipulative.

He started at a knock on the door. It was past midnight so there was only one person it was likely to be. He shouldn't let her in. Yet knowing he shouldn't was as abstract as knowing there were forty-six chromosomes in a human cell. The knowledge had no influence on his actions. No reason not to open the door to the waitress.

*Item 10. Poor behavior control.*

The next day, she went back to work and he flew back to Cambridge. As he fastened his seatbelt for landing, he wondered how he could face Tia. He turned the question over in his mind and realized he wasn't worried. He just felt he should be. The waitress—what was her name?—had put a condom on him, so perhaps it wasn't technically infidelity.

*Item 11. Promiscuous sexual behavior.*

Tia was much better tuned to what he liked, and there was no reason to let what happened a continent away stop him enjoying it.

■■■■■■

Since reading the *Time* article, Edward had spent a lot of his day staring out of his office window. Sometimes he watched the changing moods of Table Mountain or touched the plate glass window to feel the vibrations of the Southeaster blowing off the Atlantic. More often, he saw Tia reflected in it. Tia laughing. Tia frowning. Tia naked with her open arms offering an intimacy he'd never known before or since. He wondered how many girlfriends he'd discarded since Tia. Fifty? A hundred? Not one of them had kindled a flame that burned him as the memory of Tia did. What had possessed him to give her up? The answer was as obvious as the answer to introspective questions always were. He'd killed the ability to feel the flame.

He turned at a knock on the door. The art of giving his back to his callers had deserted him along with so much else.

Beatrice looked stunning. She'd replaced her cornrows with finely woven hair extensions, and her trouser suits with a high-hemmed dress revealing legs that looked as if they'd get her up to Maclear's Beacon in a dozen strides. She brought no coffee and sat without being asked.

Edward recognized the signs of the same egotism that had led him to believe he could be a CEO without Caresaway. Since he'd seen Tia's photograph in *Time*, he hadn't been able to direct himself, let alone his company.

"We have a problem," said Beatrice.

Edward sighed and faced her across his desk. Her eyes pinned him like a dead moth.

"You read the article?" Beatrice tapped her finger on the copy of *Time* that was still on Edward's desk.

He nodded. He'd reread it every day since Beatrice had given it to him, usually giving more attention to Tia's picture than the words.

"It has caused quite a stir. The FDA in America is launching an investigation. Tia de Jongh is going to help them."

Edward sat bolt upright. He was no longer able to affect nonchalance. Beatrice's features showed no reaction. Only calculation.

Something was wrong with the situation that went beyond the way Beatrice was flourishing under the influence of Caresaway. Why was she bringing him information that should have come from Pharmakaap's expensively retained lawyer?

Beatrice saw enough of him that she must have noticed moroseness drive out dominance as Caresaway drained from his metabolism. She was the only one who knew he'd no longer explode at bad news, so she'd volunteered to break it to him. Part of her job was to control access to the CEO. If she persuaded people she was the only one who could handle him, she could monopolize access to him while making herself indispensable to the rest of the board.

*Item 4. Cunning / manipulative.*

Through an act of kindness, he'd turned her into a psychopath who was rerouting the channels of power through her own desk. He edged back his chair, as though a little distance would make her less dangerous. He used to like boasting that prey always recognized a predator. Now he knew what it felt like.

"America accounts for more than half our sales," she said, "If the FDA bans Caresaway, the European Union will follow them. So will Japan and China."

All of which was true, but involved speculation above Beatrice's pay grade. She'd been talking to the other directors.

"I know a lot of our sales are under the counter," she said, "but we get paid whether the prescription is forged or not. We'll lose that business if Caresaway is outlawed. This amounts to about eighty-five percent of Pharmakaap's business. Without it, we're buggered."

It sounded like a prepared statement until the last two words, so it was probably straight from one of the other directors. She must have persuaded them she was the best person to handle Edward, and they'd agreed as readily as if she'd offered to muzzle an irate Rottweiler. The question was, what was in it for her?

"They won't close us down here," he said.

Pharmakaap had become a flagship for South African innovation. There was too much political capital to be made out of accusing foreign governments of neo-colonialism and protectionism for the government to move against them.

"True," said Beatrice, "but South Africa accounts for less than three percent of Caresaway sales."

Edward grimaced. There was no escaping the bottom line. Without exports to the USA and Europe, Pharmakaap would go back to the global minnow of a company it had been before D'Olivera bought Caresaway.

What would happen to him? Even if the board forgave him for the company shriveling up on his watch, which was about as likely as Beatrice showing him a morsel of compassion, they'd have to dump him for suppressing the side effects. He'd end up back in gray, drizzled England where he wouldn't be allowed within lying distance of any job in science. He'd be bankrupt. He couldn't understand how he'd managed to get himself into debt with the salary he'd been on for the past five years, but now he was thinking as Ed the unshaven. Edward the psychopath had been as impulsive and irresponsible as the Hare test predicted, and had blown his salary and every scrap of credit he could get hold of on his girlfriends and the Maserati.

"You should take a paracetamol," said Beatrice. "Do you have some in your desk?"

Edward had a hand to his forehead. He realized he'd just groaned aloud.

"I... I don't know." In his own voice, he heard the tone of a man past caring.

"Let me have a look."

Beatrice came around to his side of the desk. Perhaps she wasn't so far gone if she cared about his headache. She edged closer to him as she went through his drawers, brushing her hip against his shoulder. He looked up. The morning sun was low enough to throw a reflection on to the window to the admin office, so Edward saw what the admin staff saw. Beatrice was all but sitting in his lap. His right arm was out of sight, but it could be on her backside or up her skirt.

So much for compassion. She was setting up an accusation of sexual harassment. The threat would keep him under her thumb, and it would give the board an easy way to get rid of him. No tribunal would be sympathetic to a foreigner accused of being a sexual predator.

It all went through his mind in the time it took to leap to his feet and back up to the window.

"No, I cannot find any." Beatrice spoke as though nothing out of the ordinary had happened.

She walked close enough to brush past him, and jerked away as if he'd pinched her. In the admin office, two people looked away. They wouldn't wonder why he'd stood so sharply or why Beatrice had taken such a long route back to her chair. They would see what they expected to see, which was their CEO mistreating a woman.

"So what are you going to do?" asked Beatrice.

Edward sat. He wanted to go home, lock the door and wait for it all to go away. Much good that would do. Sooner or later he'd receive a politely worded letter terminating his employment, followed by less polite letters from credit card companies and banks calling in debts to pay for the institutional damage inflicted by the squabble of psychopaths running them.

"I see three options," said Beatrice. "One, we open a clinic in Antigua or St Kitts. Our American corporate customers will be able to fly there to get their pills legally. Even if the FDA bans selling of Caresaway, it will not be illegal to import prescription medication for personal use. We will have to raise the price to cover the loss of the therapeutic market, but our corporate customers can afford it."

It wasn't a bad idea as international drug smuggling schemes went, which begged the question of who had come up with it. Edward doubted she'd worked it out on her own, so there must have been other Caresaway psychopaths in Pharmakaap. As it was her talking about it in the CEO's office, she'd evidently outmaneuvered the competition for now.

"Two, you need to talk to this Tia de Jongh. I hear you were more than business partners."

Edward said nothing.

"Offer her a place on the board. That's what's bugging her, isn't it? She thinks she didn't get her due."

"I don't think that's all," said Edward.

"You can apologize for whatever you did. Get down on your knees if she wants you to, but get her on side. If she's the only one who knows about the tests - what were they?"

"Psychopath checklists."

"Nonsense. Anyway, if she's the only one who knows about them, the FDA will have no evidence without her."

"I'm not sure that's her motivation."

"What do you mean?"

"You say we can offer her money and recognition. You say she's probably pissed off with me. You're probably right, but Tia always wanted to produce a medication that would help people.

Make depressed people feel better. She'll be horrified that Caresaway is being used as it is. I don't know what we can offer her to change her mind about that."

"I can't see it. Why would she care about helping people she's never met?"

*Item 7. Lack of empathy.*

Beatrice had been on Caresaway for less than two weeks. Perhaps it was worth trying to get through to her.

"You understood when you joined us," he said.

For the first time since she'd come through the door, Beatrice didn't know what to say.

"You've read the article," he said. "You know about the psychopath checklists. What do you think's happened to you since you started taking Caresaway?"

Beatrice blinked. It was the only sign of the battle between her old and new personalities, fought with neural impulses across her limbic system.

"I have to be candid," she said. "I have made some decisions recently. I do not want to be the person I was when I worked for Anthony D'Olivera. He kept me in a subservient position because that was where he wanted me."

Edward remembered her hugging D'Olivera after the no confidence vote. She hadn't resented him then.

"I've come to believe in myself since then. I'm much happier now, and I don't want to change."

It was a textbook psychopath's response. Compassion had no traction in Beatrice's mind, so she'd brought the conversation back to her favorite subject: herself. Trying to change her mind from what she thought was best for her was as futile as trying to derail a train with a toothpick.

"You need to speak to the De Jongh woman," said Beatrice. "The Caribbean plan will do no more than mitigate our losses if the FDA bans Caresaway."

Edward didn't want to face Tia.

Beatrice's level gaze reminded him of a lion he'd seen in Kruger National Park, whose eyes had shown his contempt for technological fripperies such as the jeep in which Edward had been sitting and the phone in his pocket. Neither offered any defense against the will to use claws and teeth, and the lion had known it.

"I'll email her," said Edward.

Beatrice's expression softened enough to let him know the claws would stay sheathed for the time being.

"I will book your flight." She sounded like Edward's PA again rather than the woman who had just pulled off a coup to take over Pharmakaap.

"Okay," he said.

She stood and made for the door. "I'll get someone to bring your coffee," she said over her shoulder.

"Thank you."

She put a hand on the door handle, paused, and looked at him. "And the third option."

"Yes?"

She opened the door. "Please do not do that again."

She spoke loudly enough for the whole admin office to hear. The message was clear. The third option was if Edward didn't rescue the company, she'd get him fired for sexual harassment. Her power over him was complete.

He'd enjoyed the predatory talent conferred by psychopathy, and he'd thought D'Olivera had been an idiot to not see his maneuvers. Now he'd become prey himself, he realized D'Olivera had seen exactly what was happening but had been too decent to use the same tools to fight back.

The only tool he needed was in his desk. With the little blister pack of confidence, he could face down Beatrice and shed his remorse at what he'd done to the world. He tried to persuade himself that a few tens of thousands of corporate psychopaths taking Caresaway couldn't have caused a global recession, couldn't have put millions out of work, couldn't be responsible for the homeless bergies he blew past in his Maserati.

It got harder to convince himself with every day since the last Caresaway pill. The bad joke was that it was a good antidepressant. A short course was exactly what someone in his present state of mind needed. If the impulse to take a pill hadn't struck him in that café, he'd have made sure the side effect was well known from the beginning. If the friends and colleagues of patients had known what to look for, the Caresaway-induced psychopaths would never have taken over the world.

He didn't want to go back to Britain as a bankrupt.

No. He wasn't going back on Caresaway.

Therefore, he needed to speak to Tia. If nothing else, she was one person in the world to whom he could apologize. He closed his eyes. When everything looked hopeless to him, Tia had always known what to do.

He looked up at a knock. A young man wearing a suit so new it still bore the store creases stood on the other side of the glass door. Beatrice must have sent the newest new boy on a coffee run.

"Come in," said Edward.

The young man swallowed, opened the door, and placed the coffee on Edward's desk as though one drop spilled would detonate a bomb.

"What's your name?" asked Edward.

"Sfiso, sir."

"Well, thank you Sfiso."

Sfiso looked as though a shark had saved him from drowning.

■■■■■■■

Whether Edward had slept with fifty or a hundred women since moving to Cape Town, none had run their fingers over him with Tia's blend of desire and affection. None had made him feel sex was an adventure on which they were embarking, hand in hand. None had slid him off the crest of a shared orgasm into an embrace that was their whole world.

His mind channeled all his regrets through the memory of the last time with Tia as his heart channeled his blood. It hadn't been their best because Caresaway had already robbed him of the ability to share the joy of it, but it hadn't mattered to him because it had also taken his ability to notice.

"You're different lately," Tia had said as she snuggled to him.

Her breath had still been a little short so he'd tweaked her nipple.

She'd gasped. "Bad boy."

"So you're not complaining, then."

"No. I was starting to miss this."

He'd tugged the duvet around them. They couldn't afford to run the heating all night, and the wind-rattled window had sounded like a machine sucking heat out of the flat. Edward had settled himself with a little distance between them, and Tia had shuffled over to nestle her head on his shoulder.

He stifled a gnaw of irritation.

"Cape Town's been good for you," she said. "You must be looking forward to moving out there."

"It's not finalized yet."

"It's going to happen. They want Caresaway."

They were still negotiating the buyout and the positions he and Tia would be offered, but she was right. Pharmakaap was hooked.

"True," he said. "It's time someone wants it."

They lay in silence while Edward wondered if Tia was holding him back. Would he have sold Caresaway to one of the bigger companies if he hadn't listened to her advice on presentation? Somehow the question was linked in his mind to another. Did he want to spend the rest of his life with no other woman in his bed?

"Edki," she said.

"Yes."

"We never talked about the Hare tests."

Edward's irritation flexed its muscles, warming up for some task he couldn't yet guess at.

"Don't worry about it."

"I know we don't have a sale yet, but we do need to talk about it. We don't want to turn every stressed-out executive into a corporate psychopath, do we?"

She'd actually joked about it back then.

"I said, don't worry about it."

She put her palm against his cheek and turned his face toward her. They'd often discussed work in bed, and he'd never refused to engage before.

"What's worrying you, Edki? If you can't tell me by now?"

Tia was the last person he could tell he wanted to bury the Hare test results. She'd never agree to that.

Once he was in Pharmakaap, he wanted a place on its executive board. He needed to be associated with a blockbuster product, not one that would need years of expensive development.

Tia wouldn't leave it alone now she'd asked him. He'd have to pacify her.

"We retested all the recruits when they'd been off Caresaway for two weeks," he said. "They were back to normal."

"That's good. But some relapsed back into depression as well."

"Well, yes."

The trial had only lasted six weeks, which was about as long as conventional antidepressants took to have any effect at all. The people taking Caresaway had reported feeling much better after the first week. One woman had told Edward she'd gone to bed in monochrome and woken up in color.

"So some people will need long-term treatment on Caresaway," she said, "which means they'll be psychopaths for prolonged periods."

Trust Tia to cut to the heart of the problem.

"Better than being depressed."

"Perhaps, but what if they come off it and find they've destroyed all their significant relationships? And what about the people around them? Friends, partners, colleagues. Psychopaths are destructive."

"You've been reading."

He made it sound as if he hadn't known, although he'd seen copies of books by Robert Hare, inventor of the Hare test, around the flat.

"I'm worried about it, Edki."

He hugged her.

"I know, Tia. I'm not saying you're wrong, but let's discuss it tomorrow. Make a proper plan."

"Mm."

She'd cuddled back. "Early morning meeting. Gives us an excuse to be late to the office."

"Mm." He'd made his voice sound sleepy, hiding the excitement bubbling inside him. He felt like an explorer mapping the topography of his new personality; it took a moment's thought to recognize he was excited because his decision was already made.

*Item 13. Impulsivity.*

He didn't sleep much that night, partly because of his excitement and partly because Tia moved as she slept. Before Caresaway, her movements had nudged him close enough to wakefulness to appreciate the riches beside him. Now they annoyed him into fully waking up.

He made breakfast for her next morning. He wanted to remind her how much he'd done for her by doing one last thing. When they'd eaten, they faced each other across the kitchen table. When they started touching during a work discussion, they had more fun but nothing got decided.

"So," said Tia. "Hare tests."

"There's something else we need to talk about," he said.

"First?"

"Yes. I've been trying to work out how to tell you."

Tia frowned. "It can't be that bad, can it? It's not like you're pregnant or something."

He didn't smile. "I spoke to Pharmakaap yesterday. They offered me five million for the company and a senior post in their research and development unit. If Caresaway works out, it's a fast track to a directorship."

"That's good, isn't it?"

"Very good. I'd be an idiot not to take it."

Tia shifted in her chair. It wouldn't be until Edward remembered the moment without the influence of Caresaway that he'd attribute her discomfort to his use of the pronoun 'I' instead of the 'we' he'd always used to discuss the business.

"So why didn't you tell me yesterday?"

"Because there's a problem. They don't want you."

She flinched. "Why… why not?"

"Oh you know. It's a small firm. They can't create two posts for us, and Caresaway is more mine than yours."

He was fascinated by how easily the lie came. Tia knew the detail of Pharmakaap's actual latest offer, which included a post for her. He'd get a much better offer when he told them she was no longer interested in working for them.

"So what did you say?" she asked.

"I said yes. Like I said, I'd be an idiot not to."

The last time he'd seen that look on her face was when he'd reversed their car into a tree.

"You didn't even mention this to me? What am I supposed to do?"

"That's up to you."

"I can't believe..." She blinked several times. Perhaps she had been trying not to cry. "Edki, this isn't like you. We've shared everything for years."

He couldn't think of a reply so he shrugged.

"What's going on with you?" she asked.

"I made a decision. It was the right decision. That's all."

"No, that's not all. You're not even sorry, are you? This isn't like you. What..." She had shifted away from him. "Oh my god. You're taking them, aren't you? You've become a...a..."

"No, Tia, I'm not taking Caresaway."

The last thing he wanted was Tia telling Pharmakaap to ignore his next offer because his wonder drug had turned him into a psychopath.

"I've had to take control of myself recently. You know the state I was in. It couldn't go on. I needed to start making decisions for myself."

"We're *partners*, Edki. We're supposed to make decisions together."

He'd been right. She was trying to keep him dependent.

"You'll still get your cut of the buyout."

By the time they'd paid off their debts and the venture capitalists who funded them, his and Tia's shares wouldn't come to more than a few thousand pounds. Not much for three years' work, which was why the jobs with Pharmakaap were so important.

"And then what will I do? Follow you to Cape Town? Pick up what I can get?"

"If you want."

"If I *want*? Do *you* want me to?"

No, he didn't. That was part of the decision he'd reached last night. Perhaps he hadn't been taking Caresaway for long enough because he couldn't tell her directly.

"It's up to you."

It fascinated him to watch her face tell the story of her dying dreams, from sitting on the beach at Clifton to the children they'd talked about having when their lives were more stable. He felt an overwhelming sense of relief. He was free.

He remembered his resolution to stop taking Caresaway if he became psychopathic. He hadn't anticipated how much he'd like being a psychopath.

■■■■■■■

Since Beatrice had introduced the idea of talking to Tia, he hadn't been able to get that day out of his mind. He saw Tia's pain in the eyes of young women he passed in the street. He heard her voice in the wind blowing around his house in the small hours of the morning. He missed her smooth skin as he would a recently severed limb.

When she answered his email and agreed to meet him in London, he'd been as happy as he could be without Caresaway. If he could see her, there was still a chance he'd hold her in his arms again. The hope survived less than five seconds before shame smothered it. He'd killed all that was good in himself, and the man he was now would have to live with his choices.

It hurt that she wouldn't let him visit her at home, but then her testimony was a threat to the most powerful psychopaths in the world. His feeling of rejection was petty. He should be glad she recognized the danger she was in.

Rain whipped his face as he followed his iPhone to the café. He could no more deny the excitement at seeing her again than the dread. Edward turned into a Georgian mews with a key cutter opposite the café and a florist next to it. Two other shops were boarded up, casualties of the recession. London lived off the desiccated global finance industry as a plant lived off topsoil.

"Got a couple of quid for a cuppa tea?"

Edward looked down to see a man's face lined more by care than age, wearing a battered jacket limp with rain. This was what recession meant: ambition shrunk to the price of a cup of tea so he could sit somewhere dry for an hour or two. Edward rummaged in his pocket and gave him a twenty-pound note.

"Ta very much, squire. You're a scholar and a gentleman."

*If you knew the truth, you'd wring my neck.* He fled the gratitude into the café.

Tia was sitting in a corner where she would be hard to see from the street, and the mews was quiet enough that anyone loitering outside the café would be conspicuous. Tia had learned the habit of being careful.

She'd cut her hair short and put on a few kilos. She was so beautiful Edward nearly turned and ran.

She looked up. Her face showed no expression as she looked straight at him, letting him know she'd seen him. He sat opposite her. He was less likely to run if he was sitting down.

One of the things he missed about being a psychopath was being able to summon words and facial expressions as he needed them. Without Caresaway, his emotions ran too deep to stay hidden. Edward had rehearsed what he wanted to say a thousand times. He should explain about his disastrous decision to take Caresaway, beg her forgiveness, tell her he couldn't stop loving her, ask her to help him undo the damage he'd done with their invention.

"Hi," he said. "Quiet in here."

She pulled a recorder out of her handbag, switched it on and put it on the table.

"That's why I chose it," she said. "I want a clear transcript."

"Okay."

The recorder told him she'd gained experience in dealing with psychopaths, and that she knew he'd lied to her when he said he hadn't taken

Caresaway. She wanted to record the conversation, because psychopaths were such convincing liars that if they regretted saying something, they could make the person sitting opposite them doubt they'd ever heard it. Edward had grown used to thinking of the truth as a commodity too precious to give away in casual conversation, especially when there were better ways to persuade someone to do what he wanted.

"So I guess you're going to ask me not to talk to the FDA," she said.

"That's what I was sent here to say, yes."

"You were sent? Come on, you're the CEO. You do the sending."

There was no point in trying to explain how Beatrice had rearranged Pharmakaap's power structures.

"Well go on," she said. "Let's hear it."

"There's a job in research and development. Deputy director. You'll do most of the day-to-day management and have plenty of freedom to run your own projects. Right up your street. One point four million rand per year."

"I'm not moving to South Africa. My husband and I have bought a house here." Husband. She'd said 'husband'. He hadn't thought to check for a wedding ring but now he looked, there it was in plain silver.

"He's Colombian, so we want our child born here," she said. "A British passport's still worth having."

Edward's mouth opened and closed.

"Yes I'm pregnant," she said. "Did you think I'd just got fat?"

Something like screaming sounded in his ears.

"Stop looking at me like that," she said. "Was I supposed to have been doing nothing but pining since you dumped me?"

Edward had been so caught up in his own hopes and fears that it hadn't occurred to him that she might have married.

A waitress picked up Tia's empty cup.

"Would you like anything, sir?" she asked Edward.

He looked up. The waitress saw his face and fled.

"You'll have a backup plan," said Tia. "Let me guess, an executive directorship with a nice fat retainer in exchange for a confidentiality agreement. Am I right?"

"I... uh... yes."

"You know where you can shove that. Are we done?"

"Tia, please don't go."

"A backup to the backup plan?"

"No, no. I just want… Tia, I'm sorry. I still love you and I'm sorry."

She rolled her eyes.

"I've spent the last year talking to psychopaths about Caresaway," she said. "Most of them are more convincing than that."

"I'm not taking Caresaway," he said. "Not anymore. I'm the man you used to love."

Her gaze quartered his face. The shadows under his eyes and the lines of strain could not be the products of a psychopath's self-confidence.

"That's really true, isn't it? You're not taking it anymore."

"No."

"I always thought you were. Anthony D'Olivera said you must be, the way you pushed him out."

"I was then. That was the day I decided I was too good to need it."

They looked at each other in silence. It was disorientating to have no idea how to turn someone to his will.

"Why?" she asked at last.

It could have been a question she'd been wrestling with since the day he dropped her. It could have been a word to fill an awkward silence. It didn't matter. Everything spilled out of him in a flood. How he took Caresaway because he was terrified he'd drive her away. How he'd become a person he now despised for what he'd done to Tia, to himself, to the world he'd placed in the thrall of psychopathic executives. How he still envied that man his confidence, his gift for making people feel the way he wanted them to feel about him and above all his unshakeable comfort with who he was. How he'd stopped taking the pills in a moment of hubris.

The flood of words left him panting for breath, silently crying out for a single word of understanding.

Tia put her hands to her forehead and wiped them down her face.

"Oh, Edward. What have we done?"

Edward. Not Edki. The sound of his name hurt like a boot in the kidney.

"You haven't done anything. It was all me. All my fault."

"Do you remember the day you presented to D'Olivera? When I said I'd rather have you as a psychopath than as you were?"

Edward remembered taking his first Caresaway pill. Apart from that, everything else was smothered by the desperation he'd been feeling that day. "I don't remember."

"Well, I said it. I've had years to wish I hadn't, because that was what got you to take the pill, wasn't it?"

Edward shrugged.

"If I'd had my head about me, I'd have known it was a stupid thing to say," said Tia. "It wasn't just asking for trouble, it was sending it a written invitation and leaving the door open. So it's on me as well as you."

"I took the pill, Tia. You didn't ram it down my throat."

"Yes, you did. That's why none of that makes me any less angry with you."

"I know I've done terrible things. I'm here to ask you to help me undo them."

"I'm already undoing them. I'm meeting the FDA next week. When I tell them you suppressed the evidence that Caresaway turned people into psychopaths, what do you think they'll do?"

Disgrace. Bankruptcy. Lawsuits for every broken marriage or career that could be blamed on Caresaway. All so much more bearable than life without Tia.

"It won't put an end to Caresaway." If he could persuade her she needed him, she'd keep in touch. If she kept in touch, there was hope. "If it's banned in the US, Pharmakaap will set up clinics in the Caribbean. Executives can afford to fly there to get their supplies."

Tia frowned, showing she hadn't considered that. It took her all of five seconds to catch up.

"Of course, if rich people want something, they'll get it," she said. "But you're forgetting, psychopaths are bad for business. No one wants to recruit one, even if they're psychopathic themselves. Once there's a bit of publicity about this, psychopath screening will become an essential part of recruitment. Clinics in the Caribbean won't change that."

"Oh."

Edward should have thought of that himself. Instead, he'd been thinking about Tia and leaving Beatrice to think about the future of Caresaway.

"And the best bit," she said, "they don't need to take my word for it. Not anymore."

She tapped the recorder. "I guess that proves you're telling the truth about not taking Caresaway," she said. "No psychopath would have made that mistake."

"You thought my saying that was a *mistake*?"

"Wasn't it?"

"No. If you're going to tell some very powerful psychopaths they can't have what they want, you need me on record, agreeing with you. Anyway, the least I owe you is some honesty."

He thought about what he'd said about suppressing the Hare tests and the clinics in the Caribbean. Words that would be played on documentaries and news channels around the world. The rest of his life would be haunted by the words he'd just spoken. He'd probably regret it later, but at that moment, he was proud of himself in a way no psychopath ever could be. It was a pride in having done right by someone else instead of for himself.

"I do deserve it," said Tia. "But I guess I should thank you all the same."

It was little enough to atone for all he'd done. He couldn't find a way to say that, so he shrugged again.

She put the recorder in her handbag. His last seconds in Tia's company ticked away.

"Tia, can you ever forgive me?"

He stared down at his hands, clasped so tightly his fingers hurt.

"Maybe," she said. "Not today. Maybe one day."

Maybe. There was hope in the word. Hope that one day she might look at him with less hatred than he'd earned.

He looked up.

She was gone.

He sat. As the gray day deepened to night, a study in dejection that was his face reflected in the window coalesced over the street outside.

"Sir?" The waitress stood more than an arm's length away, as though whatever she'd seen on his face was infectious.

"We're closing," she said.

Edward lurched outside. He didn't know where he was walking but when a bus swept rain into his face, he recognized Tottenham Court Road. A second bus was coming. Ten tons at thirty miles per hour, painted the same bright red as his Maserati. He swayed toward the road as though drawn by its gravity. The sense of falling was exhilarating. No bankruptcy, no law suits, no more memories of Tia scratching in his head like a trapped rat.

No.

The slipstream sent him staggering for balance.

As long as he and Tia were both alive, there was hope. Yet hope was flimsy and suicide called to him as sports cars and tailored suits once had. How would he resist its pull through the storm about to break around him?

There was only one choice. Pharmakaap's London office would open in the morning. More than twelve hours away. With his decision made, the idea of being trapped with his feelings for that long was more than he could endure. A green cross shone outside a 24-hour pharmacy like a lighthouse to a storm-battered ship.

Edward pulled out his iPhone and flicked through a set of numbers he'd kept from D'Olivera's investigation.

"Is that Chris the Scrip?" he asked.

"So I'm told."

"I need a prescription for Caresaway. Tonight. A little bird tells me you can help."

# About the Author

DJ Cockburn is a British author with stories in Apex, Interzone, and various anthologies. His story "Beside the Damned River" won the 2014 James White Award. He has supported his unfortunate writing habit through medical research on various parts of the African continent and drinking a lot of coffee.

Earlier phases of his life have included teaching possibly unlucky children and experimenting on definitely unlucky fish. He can be found online at http://cockburndj.wordpress.com/ and has occasionally been caught twittering as @DJ_Cockburn.

# About the Publisher

Annorlunda Books is a small press that publishes books to inform, entertain, and make you think. We publish short books (novella length or shorter) and collections of short writing, fiction and non-fiction.

Find more information about us and our books online: annorlundaenterprises.com/books or on Twitter: @AnnorlundaInc.

To stay up to date on all of our releases, subscribe to our mailing list at:

annorlundaenterprises.com/mailing-list

# Other Titles from Annorlunda Books

**Short eBooks**

*Unspotted*, by Justin Fox, is the story of the Cape Mountain Leopard and the author's own journey to try to see one.

*The Lilies of Dawn*, by Vanessa Fogg, is a lyrical fantasy novelette about love, duty, family, and one young woman's coming of age.

*Okay, So Look*, by Micah Edwards, is a humorous, yet accurate and thought-provoking, retelling of the Book of Genesis.

*Navigating the Path to Industry*, by M.R. Nelson, is a hiring manager's advice on how to run a successful non-academic job search.

*Don't Call It Bollywood*, by Margaret E. Redlich, is an introduction to the world of Hindi film.

**Collections**

*Missed Chances* is a Taster Flight collection of classic stories about love, all with a hint of "the one that got away."

*Love and Other Happy Endings* is another Taster Flight of classic stories, all of which end on a high note.

*Small and Spooky* is a Taster Flight of classic ghost stories, all of which feature a child.

*Academaze*, by Sydney Phlox, is a collection of essays and cartoons about life in academia.

Made in the USA
Charleston, SC
21 January 2017

**IF THERE WA**

**SUCCESSFU**

**WHAT IF IT ALSO MADE YOU A PSYCHOPATH?**

EDWARD CROFTE WAS A DEDICATED SCIENTIST WHO SET

OUT TO DISCOVER A CURE FOR DEPRESSION. AFTER YEARS

OF WORK AND SACRIFICE. HE HAD A DRUG THAT SEEMED

TO WORK WONDERS... BUT AT WHAT COST? YEARS LATER.

EDWARD'S WONDER DRUG HAS HELPED PEOPLE WITH

DEPRESSION. BUT HAS IT ALSO HELPED DESTROY THE

WORLD ECONOMY? AND WHAT HAS IT DONE TO HIM?

nnorlunda*Books*

ISBN 9781944354190

90000 >

9 781944 354190